PRAI
THORNS OF AN

A profound tale about the difficult journey to redemption and the quest for lost innocence.

Midwest Book Review

Barbara Watkins has produced a story that held me enthralled and on the edge of my seat. *Thorns of an Innocent Soul* leaves nothing out and the unexpected twist in the tale will satisfy those who, like me, enjoy being taken by surprise.

Brian L. Porter
Author of the award-winning novel
A Study in Red—The Secret Journal of Jack the Ripper

This is a book for those who find themselves perpetually fearing Damocles' sword over their head no matter where or to whom they turn.

Reading this novella about an innocent soul is bound to touch the reader's own innocence and…look twice at one's own world.

This writer has something to say about responsibility—not just the proverbial dysfunctional story! Find out what she has to say—it's well worth it!

Viviane Crystal
Amazon top 1000 reviewer

…an amazing story of how love, hate, revenge, and total helplessness can tear you and your family apart… A must for everyone to read…

Betty Woodrum
Author of *Shattered Memories, Scattered Emotions*

ALSO BY BARBARA WATKINS

Novels
Hollowing Screams

Short Stories
Mortal Abomination
Awaken Spirit

Short Story Collections with Betty Dravis
Six-Pack of Blood
Six-Pack of Fear

Articles
A Testament To Poets
Cold Coffee Magazine

Film
BlindSide
2010 Movie Short
Zodiac Entertainment
Voice-over Monologue

THORNS *of an* INNOCENT SOUL A NOVELLA

BARBARA WATKINS

PUBLISHING

Cover design, interior design, and editing
by Blue Harvest Creative
www.blueharvestcreative.com

Movie poster appears courtesy of Zodiac Entertainment
Design © 2013 Zodiac Entertainment
www.zodiacentertainment.co.nz

THORNS OF AN INNOCENT SOUL

Published by
BNW Publishing

Visit the author at:
www.barbarawatkins.net
www.barbarawatkins.blogspot.com
www.facebook.com/Watkinsfanpage
www.twitter.com/paranormawriter
www.imdb.com/name/nm3634934/

To Selena,
thanks again for,
being a facebook friend.
hope you enjoy my work.

all my best,
Barbara
Watkins

As a writer, I will go down any dark alley, inch my way through the tightest crawl space, and feed on your every fear. I will take your sense of calm and tear it to shreds.

Barbara Watkins

I dedicate this to all that want to believe you do have to take responsibility for your actions while on this earth, to all who believe forgiveness can overpower your desire for revenge.

PROLOGUE

Every day I have to recall that fateful night. All of my memories have revealed a deceitful, manipulating, self-centered side of me. I have to accept the hurt and the grief I have caused to my loved ones. I can see their faces etched with sorrow and regret because they couldn't save me from the hell I must endure.

Nobody comes to see me anymore. It's just as well: they would always sit in silence as if they needed me to justify their pain.

For me there is no future. I will never experience true love again. I will never experience motherhood or feel the anticipation of what is going to happen next in my life. I have a strange sensation if I remember all the details about that night, why it happened, and relive the pain that I have caused those that loved me, only then will I be allowed to break free from this cold and dark, lonely place.

I always did what I wanted regardless of the consequences. I never took the time to celebrate or rejoice the gift of life. I thrived on hate and revenge.

When I was first brought here, I thought I would make the best of it, and in time, I would be able to leave. Except time is never-ending and I am forced to exist here with only my tormented thoughts to keep me company. I do not know if I will ever be released. They said I was given many chances to turn my life around, but I ignored them. I didn't know I would have to pay the consequences. Now, every day starts out the same and I relive my nightmares over and over, hoping to discover a way out of here.

CHAPTER 1

I grew up the third child of a family of four. Being the only girl, I was somewhat of a tomboy and learned quickly how to handle my brothers. My father worked for a major law firm and was away often either on business or late night meetings. He wasn't very good with parenting. How could you be if you're never there?

My mother was a beautiful woman, but people have different opinions about what real beauty is. She taught me at an early age about outer beauty. She said inner beauty was hidden so why worry about it. Your appearance is what mattered because it was the cornerstone to get what you wanted. She didn't like to be called mom or mama; she preferred her given name, Ella. I think she just liked hearing her name.

When I was about six years old, I went shopping with her. She wanted to buy a new dress for a business meeting that my father, Brandon, was having. I had accidentally put my boots on the wrong feet, but my mother didn't notice. The sales clerk did. When my mother overheard her ask me if I needed help to switch them around, she turned blood red with embarrassment. After we got to the car, she ripped them off my feet. She said if I wasn't smart enough to put my boots on the right feet then I didn't deserve to wear any.

It was the middle of winter and I had to walk barefoot from the car into the house through the freezing snow. As cold as my feet were, I could only think how sorry I was to have embarrassed her. I never made that mistake again.

My older brothers, Jerry and Steve, already knew to watch their step; however, my younger brother, Jim, was much like me. He hadn't learned yet what made her tick, but he would soon enough. He was only five and a year younger than me.

One night after taking a bath he forgot and left his towel on the bathroom rug. When she saw what he did, she called him back into the bathroom, made him take off his pajamas, and get back in the tub—only this time in freezing cold water. I wanted to do something to help him except I knew there would be hell to pay. As children, our mother reminded us time after time that we were responsible for everything we did or would do, and that our first responsibility was to her.

As my brothers became older they had their girlfriends over, although they never stayed around too long; Ella saw to that. It wasn't that she thought the girls weren't good enough for her sons; they just weren't good enough for *her*. My oldest brother, Steve, invited his first real girlfriend over for dinner, with Ella's permission of course. It was the first and the last time. I remember the young girl didn't cross her legs when she sat down at the dinner table and forgot to put her napkin in her lap. It was a minor thing, yet in my mother's eyes she lacked manners and was rude. She even went so far as to suggest teaching her etiquette. I felt sorry for the girl because no matter what she did, it would never be good enough for my mother.

She treated my dad in pretty much the same manner that she treated us kids. He could never live up to her standards. I always suspected he had another woman on the side. How else could he have coped? If she wasn't telling him to watch his weight then she was humiliating him in one way or another. I don't believe I ever heard her give him a compliment. Some women are just not cut out to be wives or mothers, and she was one of those people. She and my grandmother were very much alike.

My grandparents didn't come to visit often. My grandmother also preferred we children call her by her first name, Jackie. Our grandfather was much different. He was laid back and very quiet. Of course, he had to be; he could never get two words in. Our grandparents on our father's side died before we were born. I sometimes wondered what kind of people they were. It was always a contest between Ella and Jackie. If Ella bought a dress that was expensive then Jackie would have to buy one that cost more. They were always trying to outdo each other.

WHEN I was growing up, I always said I'd never be like my mother. I saw how she ridiculed my father and the abusive way she treated us kids—not just physically but mentally as well. Somehow along the way, I turned into her twin. The very thing I despised about her, I became. I always said I'd be more thoughtful about people's feelings and not be so quick to judge. How could I criticize somebody else when I had so many imperfections myself? There was always something wrong with me. Either I was too fat or my hair was too thin. If looks were needed to get ahead in life then I knew I wouldn't get far. Even when guys started to notice me and gave me compliments I felt they were teasing me.

It was about the time I turned eighteen that I started rebelling against my parents. It wasn't so bad with my father, but my mother had finally met her match. She'd molded my personality to fit hers. When I started going to modeling auditions she insisted on coming with me. It was a nightmare. All she did was get in the way and tell everyone how to do their job. I usually managed to sneak out without her. I'll never forget the time I was late for an audition because she'd spent two hours getting ready. The job was extremely important to me because it could have opened many doors. Of course I didn't get it and it was her fault. Yet all she could say to me was, "It just wasn't meant to be."

CHAPTER 2

Prom night in a young girl's life should be an exciting and memorable event, but mine turned into just one of many heartbreaking experiences to remember.

I didn't have many friends in school except for Chris, and we had remained close. We went through grade school together, and he was the only person I really felt comfortable around. He had grown from a cute, little boy into an attractive young man. I could be judgmental and critical about anyone—except Chris.

He came from a family that knew the meaning of being poor. He was the oldest of five children. His father was an alcoholic and could rarely hold a job for any length of time. His mother worked two jobs just to make ends meet. Chris had taken the role of being not only the big brother but also filling the shoes of his parents. His eyes were the most beautiful deep blue I'd ever seen. And behind them lay what was even more beautiful—his spirit.

Ella knew he was from a poor family and wouldn't allow him to visit. She said people like that just bring you down. We would see each other every day at school and sometimes sneak away to a movie. I wanted so badly for Chris to accompany me to the prom except I knew Ella would never allow it. Chris never had the chance to attend his last school dance. He ended up having to stay home and take care of his little brothers.

Little did I know, Ella had already made plans for me. She selected a young man named Philip to be my date. He was also extremely nice looking but that was about it. He hung out with the popular crowd. If you wanted to fit in, they expected you to wear a certain style and to like the things they liked. His mother and father were prominent surgeons at the hospital and they lived a very comfortable life. His mother owed Ella a favor and now it was time for her to cash in. Philip would be my date as payment. My mother told me more than once that he was my ticket to the good life.

She bought me one of the most expensive dresses she could find. Her reasoning was you went all out for a young man like that. I refused to wear a dress that I couldn't pick out and was informed I was lucky to even be going. She said he was doing me a favor; after all, I hadn't been his first choice.

I had a choice at that moment: stand up for myself or back down. I chose the latter. Resigned, I went upstairs and put on the dress I hated. Except what I hated even more was what I saw in the mirror looking back. Part of me died that night. I decided if I ever got out from under her spell, I would do whatever it took to regain my self-respect. Philip and I didn't have two words to say on the way to the dance. When we arrived I told him he could go his way and I would go mine.

"Don't expect me to act like your date. I didn't even want to come," I said.

"And you think I wanted to bring you here! Bringing you here was not even in my plans. If it wasn't for your conniving mother I could have picked any girl, and it wouldn't have been you, so don't act all high and mighty with me," he said staring coldly ahead.

"Well, maybe you should tell your mother to choose her friends more wisely next time and we wouldn't be in this situation."

He turned and walked away to join his little circle of friends, leaving me alone at the table. I thought about Chris and how I wished he could have been there with me instead of Philip.

I hated the pitiful looks I got as the other girls walked by my table on their way to the dance floor. I decided I'd had enough and told Philip to take me home.

From the time we got into the car, he proceeded to make small talk. He wanted to know how my modeling career was going and if I ever had to pose nude. Feeling very uncomfortable, I moved closer to my side of the car and put one hand on the door handle, looking away.

At first I was so nervous I didn't realize we were going the wrong way. When I mentioned we took a wrong turn, he said he was taking a shortcut and not to worry. As we got farther and farther away from the main highway, I began to panic. Something wasn't right about this situation. I told him to turn around or to let me out. He stopped, pulled the keys out of the ignition, and put them in his pocket. As he leaned toward me, my hand quickly tugged on the door handle and found it locked.

Philip's hand clamped over my mouth. I knew my biggest fear was about to happen. I could feel his hands groping every part of my body, and the stench of alcohol on his breath was sickening. The physical pain to my body was excruciating, but the feeling of helplessness was even more terrorizing.

My mind drifted back to when Ella had forced my younger brother into the tub of ice water. I recalled the sick feeling in the pit of my stomach and the helplessness I had felt. So I did the same thing I did that night. I closed my eyes, pretended it was a nightmare and told myself that when I woke up it never happened.

The next thing I remembered was walking into the house and up to my room. Standing in front of my door was Ella. She noticed my dress was tattered and torn. "What in the world happened to your dress? You better have a good excuse, young lady," she blurted out.

Choking back the tears I tried to explain. "Philip did this! He trapped me in the car and forced his way."

"Don't try to blame Philip for your carelessness. I'm sure you led him on," she yelled.

All I wanted to do was run into her arms, have her comfort me, and tell me she would make it all right. My thoughts were interrupted by her angrily reminding me how much she had spent on the dress, and that I didn't have respect for anything she ever gave me.

She often told my brothers and me that we were responsible for what we did and for what happened in our lives. Was I responsible? I knew I would have to handle this by myself. I apologized to my mother, and went into my bathroom and quietly got sick. This night marked the end of my innocence and changed the course of my life forever.

IT WAS the weekend, and my father had returned early from a business meeting. It was noon and I still couldn't bring myself to get out of bed. My father came up to see how I was feeling and to ask me how the dance went.

"Jen, I'm sorry I couldn't be here for your big night. Did you have a great time?"

Pushing my feelings deep down, and turning away so he couldn't see the tears, I answered, "It's over, that's all that matters."

"Look at me. Tell me what happened. Did Philip do something to ruin your big night? I'll talk to him if he did."

"It doesn't matter. It was just a dance." I was too ashamed to tell my father what really happened. It was hard for me to talk to him and I had never confided in him or asked for his advice.

Even though my father couldn't show his emotions easily, I knew he cared. I could see it in his eyes. I knew he loved us, and we loved him.

"Your mother and I are going to the cabin this weekend. Why don't you come along."

I thought for a moment before answering. This was my opportunity to see Chris. My older brothers had moved out recently and were sharing an apartment in the city. My little brother was staying over with friends for the weekend.

"I really need to catch up on my schoolwork. You know how Ella gets when I get any grade under an A."

"Yes, I guess you're right. Well, you know the routine. No company and make sure things are locked up tight before going to bed."

CHAPTER 3

With everyone gone I called Chris, hoping he would answer. Just the sound of his voice made me feel at ease. He answered and instantly knew something was wrong even though I hadn't said a word. Chris would be right over so we could talk. I wasn't sure I could tell him, nor if I wanted to. My heart skipped a beat when I heard the doorbell ring. Running to the door I flung it open. Instantly I stiffened when I saw Philip standing there instead. Pushing his way inside he slammed the door shut.

"Don't make a sound," he hissed. "You didn't tell anyone what happened, right? You know I had way too much to drink or things would not have got out of hand like that. Did you know you're the first virgin I've ever had? Always dreamed of settling down with a girl like you. What do you think?" he said, leering at me.

"How could you have the audacity to ask me something like that after you brutally raped me!" I screamed.

"As I recall, you didn't do a lot of fighting back. Maybe deep down you enjoyed it just a little," he said crudely.

Never before did I want someone dead. The entire time he spoke all I could imagine were my hands around his neck, squeezing tighter and tighter until every ounce of life had left his body.

Before I could say or do anything, the doorbell rang again. This time it was my savior, Chris. Knowing something was wrong he asked me if I wanted Philip to leave. Philip spoke up and said he was leaving anyway, and that he would call me later.

The moment the door closed behind him, I ran into Chris's arms. All I could do was bury my head in his chest and sob. He comforted me like always and said whatever was wrong we could fix. Chris didn't understand that this time it couldn't be fixed. The damage had been done, not only to my body but to my soul as well.

I was so happy to see him I said everything else could wait. Instead, we spent the rest of the day catching up and watching old, sappy movies. We didn't need to say much; the comfortable and warm feelings we had for each other spoke louder than words.

It began to grow late and Chris had to get back home. His mother was working a double shift, and he needed to be there for his little brothers. His dad was drunk again and in no shape to watch them.

Before he left, he said he needed to tell me something. "I think I've loved you all my life. I hope I'm not coming on too strong. I needed you to know. You have always been there for me when I needed you. And you've always treated me with respect. I want you to know I'll always be here for you. You know I can't give you a lot of material things, but I'll always have plenty of love for you."

I looked into his beautiful blue eyes and all my pain went away. It was like someone had lifted a boulder off my chest and breathed life back into my soul.

"Chris, I think you're the only person I've truly ever loved. I can't see my life without you in it. I know someday soon we will be together. Just don't give up on me."

He kissed me and I felt his heart beating in rhythm with mine. His touch was soft and gentle like nothing I had ever experienced before. In his arms I felt warm and safe. Philip may have taken my virginity and part of my soul, but tonight Chris touched my body and my soul with such tenderness and love that for a while I felt whole again. I wanted to stay in his arms all night except it wasn't possible. He had obligations at home. As he left he promised me in time we would have many beautiful days and nights together…and I believed him.

CHAPTER 4

That night I dreamt I was sitting in a briar patch. On one side of me was a bush of beautiful red and pink roses, and on the other side was nothing but a bush of thorns. Every time I reached for a rose the petals turned into thorns. The harder I tried to grab one the deeper the thorns around me became. Suddenly, all the roses disappeared except one and my body was consumed with thorns. Instead of feeling pain my body went numb. As I reached for a petal from the last rose it began to wither and die. At the time it didn't make any sense; however, as the events of my life began to unfold it made perfect sense.

It would be awhile before Chris and I would be alone again, but we talked at school and on the phone every chance we got. Chris didn't mention Philip to me again. It was as if he knew I wasn't ready to open up about what was going on. I think he was just giving me time to come to him. I went out of my way not to run into Philip because the mere sight of him made me ill. The next few weeks would fly by. With one test final after another and little modeling jobs on the side, I barely had time to sleep or concentrate on anything else. Graduation was just days away. I just wanted to get through it and start a life with Chris. I knew it would be rough. I knew Ella wouldn't approve, but I wasn't prepared for what happened next.

My brothers all came home the weekend of my graduation. It felt good to have them there. We were very close as young children, but I didn't see much of Steve or Jerry the last few years. They were trying to make their own lives away from Ella. Even Jimmy and I had drifted apart lately. Although he never said it, I knew he felt resentful that I didn't stand up to Ella when she was abusive toward him.

He handled it himself when he got older by staying out of the house with friends as much as he could. We never spoke of the pain we experienced growing up. It was hard enough while we were children to endure and talking about it now was even harder. I just wanted us to all be together and to pretend for just a little while that we were a loving family.

ONE THING I learned was how to pretend. I remembered one of the very few times our father planned a family outing. We drove up to our cabin during the middle of fall. The leaves were starting to change color and the lake was crystal clear.

My father wanted to take my brothers out on the lake and teach them to fish. The boat dock was not far from the cabin; you could walk on it and look over the water. While my father and brothers were fishing, Ella decided we could walk out onto the dock and watch them. I remember sitting down and letting my legs dangle over the edge when all of a sudden I lost my balance. Hanging on with one little hand I screamed for my mother. Just as she grabbed my wrist and was about to pull me up, she stopped. I could hear my father's boat getting closer to the dock and him yelling to hold on. With a tight grasp on my hand she suddenly jerked back and let go. I must have went under a couple of times before she jumped in to pull me up. The next thing I knew, my father was holding me in his arms and praising my mother for saving me just in time.

When you're little you expect your parents to keep you safe from harm. I was too young to understand at the time, and I wasn't sure how it had happened, but I knew Ella let me fall on purpose. The praise and attention she received was worth the risk she took. Ella would take many more risks.

CHAPTER 5

It was graduation day and I woke up with the stomach flu. It had been a long time since I felt this sick. It was impossible to keep my breakfast down. I wanted everything to be perfect. Ella said I was probably just nervous about graduating because I had no plans for the future.

My father spoke up and said, "Ella, if she plans to get as far away from you as possible that will be a good start." The phrase *if looks could kill* applied to that moment. As sick as I felt, I left the room so I could laugh.

We managed to make it to the ceremony just in time to hear my name called. My brothers had given me the nickname Jen, short for Jennifer, when I was younger, and I went by that almost all the time. When they called me up to accept my diploma and said *Jennifer Scott* it took a moment to sink in. I couldn't have been prouder.

I ran over to where Chris was standing and jumped in his arms. This was a day we could both be proud of—something we accomplished all on our own. Through all of our struggles to maintain some sort of normalcy in our lives, we somehow had got this far.

Although I planned to go with Chris and some of the others to an after party, I felt too sick. I barely made it to the car when Ella started in on me.

"How dare you embarrass me again like that. I told you I don't want you talking to that white-trash boy."

"You don't even know him. How can you call him that? He's been my closest friend through high school, and I'm in love with him."

"Please…you don't even know *what* love is. You haven't listened to one thing I've taught you. Love is about having money in the bank and being able to have influential friends to help you in a pinch. This boy can't give you any of that," she said with a smirk. I couldn't believe what I was hearing. *How could she be so calculating and cold? What happened to make her that way?*

We pulled into the driveway, and Philip and his parents were waiting. I knew Ella had set the whole thing up. Much too sick to show my contempt, I jumped out of the car and barely made it to the bathroom to throw up. Ella came into my room and told me to get myself together because we had guests waiting downstairs.

When I managed to come down, I saw Ella had placed me next to Philip. He just sat there with a smug look on his face as if he had no worries in the world. Ella made a toast. "Here's to Jennifer and Philip, may their futures be full of riches and grow to make us proud." It was exactly what I had expected her to say.

Finally, after two or three times of having to leave the table from feeling sick, I was excused to leave. Ella came up to my room after Philip and his parents left and told me to get used to seeing more of them. Even though I didn't care about my future, she did, and Philip was going to have a major role in it. She told me I had better forget about Chris and start concentrating on who could give me what I needed.

She didn't have a clue what I needed and never would because material wealth was all she knew. I made the mistake of saying, "If you want him to be a part of this family so bad why don't you get with him?" The look on her face was the same cold stare when she had let go of my hand at the dock and almost let me drown. I knew I was in for a tough fight, but I was prepared to fight this battle.

OVER THE next three weeks I didn't do much. I couldn't seem to get rid of this stomach bug. One of the more upscale magazines that I had worked with during their swimsuit layout called offering me a contract. They wanted me right away, and the only catch was I would have to travel quite frequently to various locations for photo shoots. All expenses paid and a hefty bonus was like a dream come true. It was my chance to get away from Ella and her controlling, manipulating ways.

I wanted Chris to be the first to know. I called him and asked him to meet me in the city at our favorite theater because I had good news to celebrate. We both got there early and decided to grab a bite to eat. I couldn't wait any longer so I told him about my good fortune.

"Chris, this is our ticket out of here. We can leave and never look back. We can finally have the life we've always wanted without any interference from Ella. And you can concentrate on your own needs. It's time your family let you go."

"You don't understand. I love taking care of my family. They need me and in many ways I need them. I'm sorry you have such a bad relationship with your mother, but don't you think it's time you both worked things out?"

"No, you don't understand. If you don't come with me we may never have this chance again. You don't know her like I do. She will do everything she can to keep us apart." I was begging him.

He said he'd always love me but the timing was wrong. It was impossible to leave his family right now. I didn't understand how he could feel that way. This was our chance to start a life together away from here. I told him he was making a big mistake and that I understood, but I needed to go. All the excitement and joy I felt earlier was gone. I refused to let him or Ella hold me back. We kissed goodbye, and we each walked away. Suddenly I felt very alone once again, but it was my choice.

SHORTLY AFTER I returned home, I broke the news to my father and Ella. You would have thought she had been the one with the job offer. She couldn't stop talking about how we needed to go shopping and that she didn't know what to pack. I told her straight to her face she wasn't going, and if she gave me any problems she wouldn't be invited to visit. For the first time I think she was speechless, but she knew I meant it. I wasn't going to take orders from her or anybody else.

I was sorry about leaving my dad. I wondered how he was going to manage with me gone and my brother barely around. At least when we were there it took some of the heat from Ella away from him. I figured he'd just stay away from home more.

CHAPTER 6

The next day as I waited for my plane to arrive, I said my good-byes to my father and my brothers. Ella reached out to me, but I turned away. Heading down the ramp, I turned around for one last look. Standing alone was Chris. I desperately wanted to run back and grab him, and take him with me. Except I couldn't. He had made his choice and I had made mine. Little did I know how that one choice would forever change many lives.

The plane landed and it couldn't have been a moment too soon. Still feeling sick all I wanted to do was get to my hotel room and relax. The magazine spared no expense. The room was beautiful. If I needed anything they left instructions to put it on their tab. They gave me credit cards to shop at the finest boutiques for whatever I needed, and I took every advantage to use them. Even though I hadn't done a lot of professional modeling, I knew how to manipulate and con myself to the front of the line. I would sabotage the other girls' dresses or makeup; anything to put them behind me so I always got the best shot.

DAYS TURNED into weeks, and I was exhausted. I was relaxing at the hotel when there was a knock at my door. I figured it was someone from the magazine and flung the door open. Instead, it was Philip with a bouquet of roses. He pushed his way in and said Ella had given him the details on where to find me. I told him he was wasting his time and money and if he didn't leave I would call security. That was when he said he had information about Chris that I might be interested in.

"Word around town is your precious, long-lost love Chris has fallen hard for a new, local gal. Rumor is it's quite serious. Don't you think it's time you forget about him and start concentrating on someone that can give you what you need?"

"Surely you don't think I could possibly want or need you! You don't have the foggiest idea what I want or need. We have nothing in common." He reminded me that we were both ambitious and liked having nice things. I started to think. Could Chris have really forgotten about me that fast? If so, he couldn't have loved me the way he said he did. Maybe Philip was right; maybe we did deserve each other. Philip's family had money and influence...the two things Ella always taught me were the most important things in life.

Philip would stay that night, but this time I wouldn't push him away. I closed my eyes and pretended he was Chris. The only way to get through this was to pretend and to tell myself it would get easier.

Two days later we went in front of a judge and said our I do's. There was no white dress, or bridesmaids...no music or flowers...only a cold, dark room, a judge...and Philip and I making a mockery out of a marriage ceremony.

IN THE next few weeks he would follow me from one shoot to the next. I kept so busy I didn't see him much. I think he liked being able to see the other models pose. I would catch him from time to time flirting with them, but it really didn't bother me. That should have told me something was wrong. Although I knew I would never love him, the wealth and advantages he could give me overpowered the bad.

STILL FEELING ill after several months, I thought it was time to see a doctor. I had some time in between photo shoots and decided the sooner I went the better. They ran the usual tests and I sat waiting for the results. When the doctor returned he informed me I didn't have a virus. I was pregnant.

I left the doctor's office feeling numb. That certainly explained my queasiness. Not only were my periods light, they were irregular, so I never gave it a thought when I missed one.

I spent the next hour sitting alone at the park. I had been with two men in my life. One I loved dearly and the other I despised. There was no way I could be sure who the father was. *How could I tell Chris?* I had the chance to explain before and didn't. He would never believe me now. If Philip was the father that would give him all the leverage over me he would need. What about my modeling career? In my mind there was only one alternative. I went back to the hotel and said nothing about it to Philip.

I knew most of the models kept fit by exercising and good eating habits, but some used other techniques. Some of the girls took various drugs to keep the weight off. I knew one of the models personally. I blackmailed her into giving me what I needed to take care of the situation. Then I made sure Philip wouldn't be around. I told him he needed to fly back home and get a few of my personal things that I had left behind. The more I lied the better I became. I had a few days off from work and decided to do what I felt needed to be done. With the pills in my hand I pondered my choice. I could put them down, and call the only person that I had truly ever trusted and loved, or I could take them and take responsibility for what happened next. I heard my mother's voice in my head as if she were standing right there: *You brought this on yourself. Now you're going to have to take responsibility and fix it.*

I must have passed out for a few hours. When I woke I found myself lying in a puddle of blood. My stomach was cramping, and I felt very weak. I called the doctor that took care of the other girls I modeled with, and he sent a car right away. He met me at the hospital, examined me, and gave me some pain medication. He said I had miscarried, but that I would be all right. I wasn't all right and never would be again. No medicine he gave me would stop the pain in my heart, but every day after that I took many drugs to try and numb it. I went through the next few weeks in a daze. I felt nothing I did would be worse than what I had already done.

CHAPTER 7

M y father called and said I needed to come home. My brother Steve had news that couldn't wait. I caught the next flight out. When I arrived at my parents' home, he couldn't wait for me to get out of the car. Steve ran up and pulled me out, swinging me around like we were children again.

"I'm getting married, little sister, and I am also going to be a father," he said. I never saw him so happy. I was sure it was hard on Ella not being the center of attention. Of course, she hated her future daughter-in-law. Her family didn't have the background or the money Ella thought they should. But she knew it was too late. Her little boy wasn't little anymore and he was going to be a father. It was something she couldn't do anything about.

"I'm so happy for you, Steve. I'm so happy you've found your one true love. Please promise you'll never let Ella come between you. We both know how judgmental she can be."

"I don't want to talk about Ella. I just want to concentrate on my and Ann's special day." I could tell by the tone of his voice I had said enough.

The wedding took place a few days later. Everything was beautiful. Ann was dressed in a gorgeous, white wedding gown adorned with sequins. Her bridesmaids wore soft pink gowns with flowing sashes. My brother looked like a prince-in-waiting in his double-breasted tuxedo. The church was filled with flowers. Rose petals were placed strategically up and down the aisle and the music of the church choir played softly in the distance.

I couldn't help but feel a little envious. It was everything I'd wished for with Chris. I had hoped to run into him since he and my brother had been close at one time. Distance had a way of changing that; something I knew all too well. I wanted to tell my brother to never take his wife for granted and to always respect her as well as himself. Except that wasn't necessary. He had always been a loving and caring big brother to all of us. Somehow, unlike me, he didn't let Ella change him.

I spent the rest of the day watching them stare into each other's eyes and wishing I could experience that someday. The future was his and I wished only the very best for him. I knew they would have a rocky road ahead of them. Since they lived close to our mother every day would be a challenge, especially for Ann. Ella couldn't stand to have anyone happier than she was. I only hoped my brother would stand by his new wife when the time came. But for now they had their new life and a precious new baby on the way to think about. I would always feel protective of all my brothers. I still felt responsible for not being protective enough when they were little even though I was also a child at the time.

TWO YEARS would pass before I would see my family again. My younger brother, Jim, would graduate and go off to college. Jerry was trying to break into the music business, and he joined a local band. They were traveling from one place to another hoping to get their big break. Steve and his wife, Ann, had a beautiful baby girl and opened up an antique gallery in the city.

My brothers would write me occasionally to keep me updated on their lives. I seldom took the time to stay in touch. I felt my career needed me more. But not a day would go by that I didn't think of Chris. I would close my eyes and picture his beautiful blue eyes and the loving way he would look at me.

Ella wrote just to inform me how well Chris was doing. She heard he had plans to start a family. Even thousands of miles away she still tormented me. When I asked about my father she would say, "He'll never change," and that she didn't see much of him.

CHAPTER 8

Philip started his second year of medical school and was putting in long hours. That was fine with me as it meant less time to spend together. One day I was extra tired and wanted to turn in early, but Philip was determined to get some things off his chest.

"Jen, I'm sure you've known for a while that I've been seeing someone else. It's not like we've been sharing a bed. You and I both know this marriage has been a joke. You could never let go of wanting your precious fantasy life with Chris. Not that I ever really cared. You would have never been able to completely satisfy me anyway. But the one thing we need to be clear on is my family doesn't believe in divorce. It's not an option. I don't care what you do as long as you're discreet." I had never considered our marriage to be out of love. I knew it was more for convenience and prestige, so nothing he said really upset me. I felt nothing, not pain or jealousy, nor even anger. That changed with his last confession.

"I suggest you take extra precautions on not getting pregnant. A pregnancy would be hard to explain since I was stricken with mumps as a child and left sterile." It was like someone took a sword and stabbed me through the heart. I felt my legs grow weak and suddenly I was sick to my stomach. I barely made it to the bathroom before getting sick. Finally my questions and fears were answered. The life that had been growing inside of me was from the only man I ever loved. By taking what I thought was the only way out, I not only lost Chris but the life we had created together.

Philip's revelation added to my path of destruction. The months that followed were a blur. He spent most of his nights away. I took so many drugs to dull the pain I could no longer focus on my career. As much as I hated to see Ella, I wanted to go back home. I missed seeing my dad and my brothers, but I also wanted the chance to see Chris. I booked the next flight out and headed home.

I HARDLY recognized the place. Ella changed the gate to the entrance of the house and it was now a large iron gate. The beautiful rose bushes were replaced with large shrubs. The swimming pool that my brothers and I spent countless hours in as children was now a tennis court. I wondered whom she was trying to impress now.

When I went inside the first thing I noticed that was different were the family pictures that used to line the wall leading up the staircase. They were replaced with expensive artwork. It was clear Ella was busy spending father's money. Nothing looked the same; she even turned my bedroom into a guestroom. I had left some artwork from school and a few old stuffed animals when I moved away. I wondered if she hid them in the closet so I began to look inside. In the corner I found a box with my initials.

What I found was more than I bargained for. It was full of love letters addressed to me from Chris. I sat down on the edge of the bed and began to read. In them he expressed how much he loved me and missed me. In one of the letters he wrote he had found a relative willing to move in to help him and his mother. He said it would give him an opportunity to focus on his own life. He didn't want to lose me and would follow me wherever I needed to go if I still wanted him. All I could think about was how different my life would have been if I knew about his letters.

Ella knew the way I felt about Chris. *Did she despise me enough to sabotage the rest of my life?* How could she have hidden those letters from me! Ella came in just as I was reading the last letter. Realizing what I found she tried to explain why she kept them from me. She said Chris brought them to her shortly after I had left because he didn't know how to reach me and asked her to send them to me. Knowing the way Philip felt about me, she didn't want me to make a mistake by leaving him for Chris. Ella said he had nothing to offer me and kept the letters instead because she felt it was in my best interest. She said Chris was married now, and I should forget about him.

I told myself when I moved away I would never let her torment or hurt me again. But the pain she caused this time was unbearable. I had to find Chris and let him know what she did. I wanted him to know I still loved him and to ask for another chance. I didn't care that he was married or that he had moved on with his life. All I knew was what I wanted, and I would do anything to get it.

I COULDN'T stay in the house with Ella one more minute, so I gathered my things and left. I got a room at the hotel in town and started going through the directory. To my surprise it didn't take long to find his address. I rented a car and drove to his house, parking just across the street. I was about to get out of the car when I saw Chris walk out onto his front porch. Following close behind was a beautiful girl with long, blonde hair. I watched as she put her arms around him and gave him a passionate kiss, and then she turned and went back inside. Chris waved goodbye to her as he was leaving. I followed him to the city where he stopped at a flower shop. I waited till he came out and made my move. He almost dropped the beautiful roses when he saw me.

"It's been a long time," he said.

"It's been too long," I replied.

"I got married, Jen. It took awhile to find love again but I did. She's a lot like you. I think you would like her."

"I don't know what to say, Chris. I'm happy for you. She's a lucky girl. I would love to meet her sometime, but I was really hoping we could spend some time alone. I just need a friend to talk to. Maybe we could just go have a drink."

"Tell you what. Give me your number and later tonight maybe we can have a couple of drinks and catch up on old times."

"I'm staying at the hotel in town in room 201. I'll be there most of the night. I look forward to your call. It's really good to see you again," I said eagerly. I wanted to throw my arms around him and never let go. It broke my heart to see him walk away.

Several hours went by, and all I could do was pace the floor waiting for his call. Finally it came. He agreed to meet me at the hotel. I went over and over in my mind what I would say. All I really wanted was to hold him and to feel his lips against mine. I wanted to tell him that I had never stopped thinking about him and how badly I had messed things up in my life. I ordered room service for two and some of the hotel's finest champagne. I wanted everything to be just right. This was going to be our night and no one, not even Ella, could ruin it.

I thought my heart would jump out of my throat when I heard the knock at my door. I felt like a schoolgirl again on her first date. I opened the door. Not only was the love of my life standing there but obviously the love of his life too. They stood arm-in-arm. I remembered that day I followed him home and watched from across the street. She had walked out on the porch to see him off. At the time I thought she was a pretty girl; however, now I could see she was clearly a beautiful woman.

"Hello, Jen. I'm so glad to finally meet you. Chris has told me so much about you. I must say you're even more beautiful than he described you. I hope we can become friends."

"You're embarrassing me, but Chris always had a habit of exaggerating things. I do appreciate the compliment." Chris suggested we go downstairs and have a drink. They didn't notice the dinner for two or the champagne I ordered.

Torn with the emotions of jealously and wanting to hate her, I could tell by the tone of her voice she was being sincere.

The next two hours were filled with small talk. Marty was curious and wanted to know how it felt to lead a high-fashion model's life. I lied and said, "I couldn't be happier."

We reminisced about our high school days, laughing about how we used to sneak away to see each other. Oddly, I felt very comfortable around Marty. I believed under different circumstances we could have been good friends. Chris ordered champagne; they had great news to share. Marty was three months pregnant. I literally felt the knot forming in my stomach. She was living the life that should have been mine and carrying the baby of the only man I had ever loved.

I thought of our baby I had so selfishly destroyed and the life I could never have. At that moment, I knew my hopes and dreams about a life with Chris were gone. I couldn't tell him what I had been going through or that I needed him more than life itself. Tears welled up in my eyes as I congratulated them both. I asked Marty if they had a baby girl to name her after me. I explained I wasn't feeling well and suggested the champagne had gone to my head. Excusing myself, I gave them my address to keep in touch. We hugged and promised we would.

I barely got to my room and made it to the bathroom before getting ill. What did I have to live for? I had nobody to share my life or to tell my hopes and dreams. The one thing I had was my mother, Ella. I had her to thank for ruining every chance I had at happiness. I wanted her to feel exactly how I felt—alone and desperate. I began to think how I could get back at her for everything she had done to me. It was the only thing keeping me from ending my life. I decided to take an extended leave from work and to immediately head back home again. I didn't know what my plan was. I just knew I would do everything in my power to ensure her life was miserable.

CHAPTER 9

The next day I packed up, checked out of the hotel, and headed home. Everyone was gone when I arrived. The maid informed me that Ella was out shopping, and my father had an early business meeting and would return later. I was excited to learn my brother Steve and his family would be there for dinner. It had been a long time since I saw my him and I had never seen my niece. I wanted to talk to him about my feelings and get advice, but I wasn't sure if I could.

I went upstairs to the guestroom and began to unpack. The sound of laughing outside caught my attention and I pulled the curtains open to peer outside. On the lawn was my brother and a beautiful baby girl. Excited, I quickly ran down the stairs to see them and ran straight into Ella. She was shocked to see me and wanted to know why I was home. I smiled and said it was time to put our differences aside and try to be a family again. I really wanted us to become close.

Ella had taught me very well in the art of lying and manipulating people. I knew if she thought I was sincere she would let me stay. It would give me time to calculate my revenge. It was rather unnerving how pleased she was to see me. I had expected to be interrogated with questions. Instead, she welcomed me home and said all was forgiven. Like I needed forgiveness from her! She was the one that should be begging me for forgiveness. I vowed someday soon she would.

I HAD known my father had a mistress for some time and I knew I could use this to my advantage. Long ago when I was younger, I remembered being in the city with friends and coming out of the movie theater. Up the street I saw my father with a very attractive woman going into one of the finer hotels on the strip. Although it made me sad, I didn't blame him. Ella was cold and never gave him the respect or love he deserved.

My father was an absent parent throughout most of my childhood and adolescence; however, he never ridiculed or inflicted pain upon me like Ella did. I always knew he loved me. He just had a hard time showing his emotions that way.

I was also sure Ella didn't have a clue about the affair. In her mind there was no reason my father would ever stray, and it would be impossible for him to find anyone as beautiful or as perfect as she thought she was. I was positive it would devastate her to know the truth. And that was exactly what I planned to do. As much as I loved my father, my disgust and hatred for my mother was stronger. I had a plan.

My father called and said he was running very late and wouldn't be home for dinner. He said not to wait up, but I was sure I knew what was really keeping him. We all sat down in the dining room; it seemed like forever since I had been at the family table. I was pleased my brother was there.

Steve asked how my career was going and how Philip was getting along. I smoothly covered up the truth and said he was fine, had too much work to do, and couldn't get away. I explained I was on hiatus from modeling and would return whenever they called me back. Expertly, I changed the subject back to him as I often did to get the focus off me and asked how his business was doing. As usual it didn't take long for Ella to let us know she was being ignored and wanted our attention.

"Doesn't anybody care what I've been doing lately?"

"Of course we do, Mother," my brother said, trying to sound interested. "We would love to hear what you've been up to."

"If you didn't notice, hanging on the wall going up the staircase is a one-of-a-kind, original sixteenth-century painting. I acquired it last week at the art gallery auction in Dallas. Your father threw a fit when he found out how much I paid, but he doesn't know what true art is worth."

It was the last thing we wanted to hear—Ella bragging about how much of our father's money she blew on material things to make her feel important. It didn't take my brother long to make excuses to leave early. I told Steve I would be in town for a while, and I would visit before I left.

The next day came early. I stayed awake most the night trying to plan just the right strategy to ruin my mother's life. I decided to follow my father and get his routine down so I could plan the best time to catch him with his mistress. I needed to be there to witness the hurt expression on Ella's face.

For the next three weeks, I hung onto Ella's every word and complimented her every chance I got. I wanted her to feel that we were becoming closer. I also followed my father on several occasions and watched him with his mistress. Most of the time they went to the same location at about the same time every day. All I needed to do was pick the right time and make sure Ella was with me.

Not able to wait any longer, I invited Ella to go shopping with me in the city. I selected a restaurant across the street from the hotel where I knew my father and mistress would be. I wished for luck and made sure we got a table by the window with a perfect view. I refused to miss a step and everything was in perfect order for my plan.

After we ordered our food, I looked up. There they were; walking arm-in-arm coming out of the hotel. I wasn't sure if Ella had noticed so I casually remarked, "Doesn't that look like Father standing in front of that hotel?"

The look on her face was priceless. I don't think I ever saw her face turn that shade of red before. Not wanting to show any emotion, she simply shook her head and said, "No, dear, but he does favor your father." She remarked the service was too slow and we should leave.

"Are you sure, Ella? We haven't got our food yet. Don't you want to wait? I heard the food here is delicious and one of a kind."

"I'm not that hungry anymore," she said in an agitated voice. I knew it was eating her up inside. She couldn't wait to get home and call my father. Of course, he wasn't there. His secretary said he was in a meeting all afternoon and would call as soon as it was over.

Ella moped around the house for the next couple of hours. I kept bringing up how much the man we saw outside the hotel was a dead ringer for my father. I had to keep rubbing it in. The more time passed, the more anxious Ella became. She said there were errands to run and she wouldn't be gone long. I knew it was just an excuse to check up on my father. Just as she was about to walk out the door, we heard his car pull up. I started to feel nervous and anxious. With all my planning, I hadn't been prepared to see or accept the pain and grief my father was about to endure.

Ella met him at the door. Standing at the top of the stairs I couldn't hear everything that was being said, but I could tell from their voices it was getting heated. The next thing I heard was the front door slam. I looked out the window and saw my mother peel out of the driveway. It wasn't like her to leave an argument. She loved confrontation. I lay on the bed wondering what was going through her head. *Was she feeling betrayed and belittled?* For a woman that always had the upper hand and always got everything she wanted, even if it meant stepping on everyone along the way, I was sure she must be feeling desperate and alone. In a dark and sadistic way that thought brought me much pleasure.

CHAPTER 10

A loud clap of thunder jolted me awake. I wasn't sure how long I had been sleeping. Watching through the curtains of the guest-room window, I expected to see the limbs of the huge oak tree sway-ing. Instead, I heard a blood-curdling scream. It was like something out of a horror movie. I froze; my legs felt like they were stuck in cement. I felt like I was moving in slow motion as I walked down the hall toward the sound of screams. My parents' bedroom door was open wide. On the bed lay my father and he was covered in blood. Ella screamed to get help and said he was dying.

I grabbed the phone and dialed 911. Everything was a blur and the next thing I remembered was sitting with Ella in the emergency waiting room. A nurse came out and called my mother's name. As she walked away with the nurse, I could see she was covered in my father's blood. I felt like I was outside my body looking down. I couldn't feel my heart beating; time felt like it was standing still. None of this made sense. *What happened to my father?* This had to be a nightmare.

I wasn't sure how long I was there, but finally Ella appeared. She told me to prepare myself because she had terrible news. Calmly, and with no emotion, she informed me that my father was dead. She spoke as if reading from a script. Ella said earlier that night he had been extremely depressed and admitted thoughts of suicide. She said he had mentioned contemplating suicide many times and she had begged him to get professional help to no avail.

I ran out of the hospital and fell to my knees on the pavement. I gave up praying to God long ago, and that night was no different. I questioned if there was a God, how could he let this happen? I would gladly have taken my father's place. My only reason for living was to make Ella's life a living hell. I remembered saying if there was a God and he was listening, I knew Ella was lying. She was responsible for my father's death and I vowed to be responsible for hers.

Ella made sure my father's death would not be investigated. She had a way of handling things like that. He left everything he owned to her, including a large life insurance policy. Although this might come as a surprise to some, it came as no surprise to me. She had been his first love and was still the mother of his children. In my heart, I knew he could never believe she was the true essence of evil. I thought it odd he left no burial arrangements. Ella said he told her in the case of his death he wanted to be cremated. I was sure it was just another one of her lies and to conveniently cover up the cause of his death.

THE DAY was dreary. There were no birds chirping and the sky was filled with angry, dark clouds. The air was cold and all the beautiful flowers that had once been in bloom were now dead. The cemetery was filled with friends and employees of my father's. As I looked around I saw her. Standing far behind everyone was my father's mistress. Clearly grief-stricken she could hardly keep her composure. She obviously loved my father a great deal. It gave me comfort to know maybe he finally had felt what it was like to feel truly loved, if only for a short time.

I looked at my brothers and felt sad. I knew they had to be not only mourning our father's death, but also feeling the loss of never really sharing his life. And as I looked at my mother standing there, I felt a different kind of emotion—one of loathing, hatred, and disgust. My brother Steve insisted our father be buried next to our grandparents. I was sure Ella gave in only in hopes of running into my father's mistress and causing a scene.

As we each walked by our father's casket we laid one beautiful rose on top. It had always been his favorite flower. He often commented how strange it was that something so soft and beautiful to touch could also cause such pain if not handled with delicate care. I remember thinking my life was much like that rose only without the beautiful petals. My mother was too busy soaking up all the attention to realize her main target, my father's mistress, had slipped away quietly.

My brothers and I drove the long road back to what we had called our home. Although we never had experienced a real home life, we all agreed without our father here we would never have the chance. I decided to open up and tell my brothers how Ella had been trying to sabotage my life. I told them how she hid the letters from Chris and manipulated me into marrying Philip. How I had no doubt she caused our father's death. I explained that I knew about my father's indiscretions and had purposely set Ella up. I didn't realize by pouring out my soul and presenting our mother as the monster she truly was that I would end up alienating myself.

My plan backfired. My brothers blamed me for our father's death. They said if I wasn't so hell bent on ruining our mother's life I would have considered the consequence it would have on our father. They said if our father didn't take his own life, and Ella was responsible for his death, I was equally to blame. Not only had I lost my father in death; I had now lost my brothers' love as well.

After they left I sat alone in my room thinking about what they said. *Could it be true? Should I feel partly responsible for my father's death? Had the revenge I so desperately wanted and lived for caused such pain?* How could they compare me to that monster we call our mother! She had warped their minds, turned them against me, and made it seem as if I were to blame. My hatred for her was stronger than ever. She had caused me nothing but pain and suffering all my life.

I wasn't about to take responsibility. They were just upset and didn't realize what they were saying. In time they would understand and join me in helping to destroy any kind of life Ella tried to have. After all, she'd abused and humiliated them as well. They had to feel the same way I did. They just weren't strong enough to stand up to her...but I was. I felt it was my place now more than ever to look out for them. It would take time; however, I was sure I could win their trust back.

I WAS exhausted. All I wanted to do was sleep, but I wasn't sleeping much since my father died. Whenever I shut my eyes I heard the sound of thunder ringing in my ears. Except it wasn't thunder; it was my father's gun going off. I couldn't be in the same house with my mother any longer. I decided to pack some things and go up to the cabin.

I needed to try and figure out my next move. Before I could get out the door the phone rang; it was Philip. He had heard the news about my father and wanted to know if I needed him there. I informed him there wasn't enough room for all three of us—meaning him, his girlfriend, and me—then I hung up.

CHAPTER 11

The trip to the cabin was a long one, but I knew it would be peaceful and quiet. I had forgotten how isolated it was. After driving a few miles up some winding dirt roads I could see the boathouse and the lake. As I got my things from the car and started up toward the door an eerie feeling came over me. I wasn't quite sure what to make of it. I wasn't really afraid. It was almost like I was being welcomed. I forgot how beautiful it was here this time of year.

The leaves had turned a beautiful orange and the moonlight shining on the lake cast off all the gorgeous colors. With no one around for miles and no phone to be bothered with, I could surely get some rest. After settling in, I decided to walk down the boat ramp to look out over the lake when I got a feeling I wasn't alone. Any other time I would have been frightened except it was almost a reassuring feeling. As I walked down the boat ramp it reminded me of the times my father and I used to take the same walk. There were only a handful of fond memories as a young child, but those few I treasured and no one could take that away.

When I walked back to the cabin I was exhausted. I ran a hot bath and prepared to relax. Suddenly, I heard a violent knock at the front door. I scrambled out of the tub and grabbed my robe. Who could it possibly be? No one knew I was there. I slowly and quietly crept down the hallway toward the front door. My hands sweating and my heart racing, I tried to peek through the curtains to see who was there. Looking down on the steps in front of the door, I was shocked. It appeared to be a young child huddled in a fetal position, soaking wet and sobbing. What was even more disturbing was the feeling I knew this child.

After what seemed to be an eternity, I finally got the dead bolt unlocked and I threw the front door open only to find myself looking at an empty step. Shocked with disbelief, I just stood there looking out in the dark. The phone rang and I almost jumped out of my skin. I ran back inside to answer it, only to hear what sounded like a man's voice in a low, soft whisper say, "My darling, forgive and let go of the past for only you can save that little girl, or you can let her tormented soul haunt you for eternity."

Suddenly, I felt emerged in ice water. My body ached from the cold. I opened my eyes to find myself naked in the tub of water I had prepared hours earlier. Frightened and confused, I managed to pull myself up out of the tub. I walked to the door to find the dead bolt was still locked. I nervously peeked out the window only to see the sun shining. I now realized it had to be a nightmare. The knock at the door, the small child wet and sobbing on the steps, the phone call—all of it had been a frightening nightmare. It all seemed so real. *What did it mean?* I never had a nightmare that was so vivid. In the nights to follow at the cabin, I would have many more disturbing dreams. Each and every one becoming more detailed.

One reoccurring dream was about the incident that happened to me at the lake when I was a child. I always felt if my father and brothers had not been there then Ella would have let me drown. I had tried for many years to bury those haunting memories deep within me but now they were resurfacing in my dreams.

I DROVE back to the city to pick up a few things I needed from the market. As I made my way around the market I ran into Chris and Marty. She was now starting to show. She had that beautiful glow that some women have when they are pregnant and it made me green with envy. Chris was as handsome as ever. I had hoped with time I could look at him without my heart feeling like it was breaking in two but it would never be. I thanked them for the beautiful card and flowers they sent to my father's funeral. They couldn't attend because Marty was sick from her pregnancy.

"I am so sorry about your father's passing, Jen. He was a good man. I know he wasn't around a lot when we were younger, but when he was, it was clear how much he loved you and your brothers."

"That means a lot to me and I want to believe it's true. I want you to understand that I don't think my father took his own life."

"What are you saying? Do you think it was an accident?"

"No, Chris. I believe his death was by my mother's hands."

"I know how you feel about your mother, but surely…well, you can't possibly think she did such a thing!"

"You don't know her or what she's capable of. I tried to tell you years ago except you wouldn't listen to me."

"Can you prove it? Is there solid proof you can use against her? You know you can't just go by what you think happened."

"No, sadly there isn't solid proof, but I know in my heart she is responsible. And that's something I'll have to live with."

"I hope this is one time you find out you are wrong. If you need anything all you have to do is ask." But what he didn't understand was what I needed he wasn't able to give me. I thanked them both and hurried out of the store.

When I returned to the cabin I decided to keep myself busy by repainting some of the rooms. I never really liked the color scheme my mother had chosen, so I decided to brighten it up. I got halfway through painting the kitchen when I decided to take a break. The fumes were getting quite strong. I poured a glass of wine and stepped out on the terrace. The night air felt good and the quiet was peaceful. All of a sudden I had the same feeling I felt when I first arrived at the cabin. A sense that I wasn't alone; it was a comforting feeling, not disturbing. Then a sweet, powerful aroma filled the air like roses. It made no sense; there weren't any flowers in bloom this time of year. Then it hit me. Was this my father's spirit?

I had heard about things like that but never put much thought into them. I believed that when you died that was it. I never was into fortune-tellers or was curious what might be after life.

Our family wasn't religious, and I couldn't recall as children ever going to church. Ella did all the preaching. Although my father had been curious. I remember him purchasing different books on religion, but I never was really interested enough to read them. I came to the conclusion that the combination of stress and the fumes from the paint made more sense. I finished painting the kitchen and was too exhausted to even shower.

I lay on the couch and hoped this night would be different. I longed for a dreamless night except it was not to be. Once again, I was tormented with visions—the near drowning as a child, people with blacked-out faces, my father lifeless on his bedroom floor. I dreamed of holding a precious baby in a hospital room only to have it taken away by faceless figures. It only made me ache more for Chris and our baby that I had so selfishly destroyed. I couldn't understand why I was being tortured with these visions. *Why now?*

All I ever wanted was Chris and a chance to have a family with a normal life. If there was a higher being or a God, why did he let all these terrible things happen? I didn't blame God. I blamed my mother. She was always at the beginning, the middle, and the end of everything in my life that had caused me sorrow and pain. I wasn't about to forgive or forget.

CHAPTER 12

I spent most of the next day sitting around in a daze. I couldn't remember the last time I had actually slept through the night. Did I even have a career left to go back to? I didn't care enough to call and find out. All my focus was now on ruining my mother's life. I remembered Ella had despised Ann, my older brother Steve's wife. Ella believed she got pregnant and tricked him into marriage, which wasn't true. Ann's family didn't have the money or prestige that Ella considered fitting for her son's hand in marriage.

I decided to pay a visit to my sister-in-law. I was sure there was no love lost on Ann's side either. Maybe she knew some dirt I could use on my mother and might possibly be interested in helping me. I would use anybody if it benefited me in anyway—especially if it meant destroying my mother.

I pulled up in front of my brother's home and was somewhat surprised. I didn't expect such an extravagant house. I wasn't aware that an antique shop brought in that kind of money. It was a huge three-story home with giant pillars in front. The landscape looked like it was professionally done. I couldn't wait to see the inside.

Although Ann was surprised to see me, she kindly welcomed me inside. It was just as beautiful. Of course, most of their furnishings were antiques they had acquired. Ann said the baby was napping and asked if I wanted to go out by the pool. I sensed she was nervous about something. She informed me my brother would not be happy if he knew I was there. He had told her about our conversation after my father's funeral. She said he was still upset with me, so I told her I wouldn't be there long. We sat down and I explained why I thought Ella was responsible for my father's death, as well as some other things she had got away with in the past. I didn't go into great detail, just enough.

"Jen, I understand why you feel your mother was capable of committing such a horrible act. Your brother opened up to me shortly after we were married and told me of the terrible abuse you children endured. It was heartbreaking." I knew right then at least one person was on my side. I was thankful my brother was truthful with his wife about our abusive mother. She told me my mother tried many times to break up their marriage.

"One time your mother hired a couple of lowlifes to lie and say they had slept with me, trying to get your brother to doubt he was our baby's father. Of course it didn't work, but she wouldn't give up trying to do anything to cause trouble."

"I'm sorry, Ann. I'm sorry you've had to endure her torment. It's not enough she tormented us as children, but she continues to try and ruin our adult lives as well."

Just as I felt she had more to tell me, the sound of my brother's voice echoed from the front of the house. I gave her my cell phone number and told her to get in touch with me as soon as she could, and we would continue where we left off. When I left I went around back so I wouldn't run into my brother. I wasn't ready for a confrontation, not just yet.

BACK AT the cabin, I thought about everything Ann told me. Ella was never going to quit hurting people. It wasn't enough to hurt and devastate her own children, she also had to destroy or get rid of anyone who loved them. Could she be that sadistic? Of course, she had proved that many times. I thought about the last night my father was alive. Where did Ella go when she left so suddenly that night? *Had she put the gun to my father's head and pulled the trigger? Could she have been so desperate? Was she afraid my father would leave her and take his money?* I thought it possible. In fact, I thought it most likely. I knew I would never be able to prove her guilty beyond a doubt, but there was no doubt in my mind. I would be her judge, and before my life was over I would sentence her the way I saw fit.

Everything that happened in my life, all the sadness and the disappointments, led up to this point in time. There was no turning back. If there was I couldn't see it. I was in a very dark place. I felt disconnected from everything that had meant anything to me. I wasn't afraid of going to hell. I felt I'd lived there since I was born. What did I have to lose, my sanity? I lost that long ago.

I thought if I destroyed my mother maybe I would finally have some peace. Maybe the nightmares would stop. Did I want her dead? She was already dead to me. I wanted to see her alive and in as much pain as she had inflicted upon me. How did I get to this dark, meaningless point in my life? Because Ella had dragged me here. I remembered something my father had once said to me that he read in one of his religious books, "Behold, mother is the name for God on the lips and in the hearts of all children." I wish I understood what that meant.

After another sleepless night, I sat around most of the morning waiting for Ann to call. I decided to go into the woods and bring back some small pieces of wood to burn in the fireplace. The weather had become colder since I first arrived. I gathered what I could carry back and started toward the cabin. Although I didn't walk far it was already getting dark. Somehow, I got turned around and couldn't remember which direction I needed to go. I knew I couldn't panic or I would be in trouble. I didn't bring my cell phone or a flashlight because I didn't think I would need them. The harder I tried to focus on which way I needed to go, the more disoriented I became.

I must have walked for hours. It was so dark by now I couldn't see a thing, and my hands and toes were beginning to sting from the cold. All of a sudden out of nowhere I saw a faint light in the distance. I began to follow it as fast as I could. The closer I got, the brighter it became. Then I heard a man's voice yelling for me to stay put, he would be right there. Frightened, I knew he was my only hope of getting out of there before I froze to death. "Little lady, what are you doing out here at night by yourself?" he asked. In front of me stood a young man wearing a backpack and carrying a lantern.

I had never seen this man before, so I replied, "I could ask you the same question."

"My buddies and I were just camping out down the road. We heard there were some nice hiking trails around here and we didn't see any trespassing signs posted. Hope we're not intruding!"

"No," I said nervously, "you just startled me. I wasn't expecting to see anybody else up this way. Especially this time of night."

"So, is that your cabin just up the trail?" he asked.

Hesitant, I answered, "Uh…yeah. Me and my family come up here quite often. I should be getting back."

"Would you like me to follow you back? It's easy to get turned around out here, especially at night," he said.

"No, I'll be fine. I guess I just panicked and got turned around."

"Okay then, we'll be right down the path. If you get into trouble again just yell." I hurried on down the path, and back to the cabin.

I nervously locked the door behind me and watched out the window for any sign of movement in the dark. How strange. In all the time I had been coming up here I never saw another person in this area. At the time I didn't give it that much thought. I was just glad I ran into him when I did, or I would have froze to death. I chalked it up to a strange coincidence and left it at that. Even stranger, tonight was the first time since I arrived that I actually slept all night.

I woke up thinking about the young man. What was he really doing in the woods? I decided to track where I went and take a look around. This time I took my cell phone and my flashlight. I started with my tracks that led into the woods. There was only one set of footprints and they were mine. There was no sign of campers being in that area at all. I decided to go back and get the car so I could drive around the area to get a better look.

JUST AS I started back, my cell phone rang. It was Ann; she wanted to continue the conversation we had started the day before. I suggested we meet at a small diner a few miles from the cabin. I was excited to hear what she had to tell me.

A short time later we sat down, ordered a couple of drinks, and she began to tell me a disturbing story. Ann said one night Ella had volunteered to watch their baby, Mandy, so that they could go out and have an evening alone.

"Your mother insisted on coming to our home. She said it would be easier to watch the baby here. I didn't like the situation to start with. Your mother hadn't taken an interest in her grandchild up until then. But I went ahead and agreed. I gave her specific instructions to take extra precautions if she went out by the pool. I told her Mandy was just beginning to take her first steps and the pool fascinated her.

She assured me everything would be fine and not to worry. But in the middle of our dinner I got the strangest feeling something was wrong. We tried to call home but got no answer."

Suddenly, Ann stopped in the middle of her story. I could see she was extremely upset. I told her to take her time. After taking a breath and trying to contain her emotions, she continued. "When we arrived an ambulance was parked out front. We didn't know what to expect. When we reached the house, we walked in and found Ella sitting calmly on the couch. A paramedic was holding Mandy, trying to comfort and calm her down. They reassured us everything was going to be okay. Ella said she had just turned away for a moment to answer the phone when Mandy fell in the pool. She said she grabbed her out immediately and began CPR. Even the paramedics were praising her for acting so quickly. I didn't believe it for a minute. My gut instinct was telling me she had almost let our baby drown. And I don't believe for a minute that it was just an accident. But your brother wouldn't even discuss it. I think he couldn't bear to know the truth."

Ann said she felt Ella was letting her know how easy it was to make something look like an accident. That was the last time Ella was ever left alone with their baby. Ann said that a short time later Ella gave her son a gift; a substantial amount of money for them to redecorate their home. She said she knew it was just a bribe to win back her son's trust.

I was speechless. *Could she have done this terrible thing to her own grandchild?* Why not, I thought. She had done almost the same thing to me years earlier when I was just a child. I agreed with Ann. She was giving her a warning. Most likely hoping it would scare Ann enough to leave her son that way she could pick out his next companion, one that lived up to her standards.

It takes a somewhat evil person to think like one, and I was becoming better at it every day. I told Ann not to worry. I had a plan to deal with Ella, and she wouldn't ever have a chance to hurt anyone else. I could tell Ann was shocked and confused but didn't ask any questions. We said our goodbyes, and I headed back to the cabin.

CHAPTER 13

The truth was I didn't have a plan. I couldn't use anything Ann had told me against Ella, but it did justify everything I already knew about my mother. She would stop at nothing to get what she wanted. I came to the cabin for a specific reason. I needed to get away from everyone and to plan my revenge on Ella. Between the nightmares every night, no sleep, and the unexplainable occurrences that kept happening, I didn't have the strength or mental capacity for it.

I couldn't get the vision out of my mind of my brother's baby girl helpless in the pool. I could see my mother tossing her little body in the water and then pulling her up only to push her back down again. I could see her little body gasping for air and Ella standing there with that sadistic smirk on her face. She was truly evil in the worst form.

I thought of those mothers I read about in the paper and saw on the news that hurt their children, or would make them sick, and then get them medical care, all for their own amusement and attention. Of course when caught in their diabolical act, they would get a doctor and hire a lawyer to come up with some ridiculous medical condition to excuse their inconceivable actions. Ella fit perfect in that category, along with all the other psychotics. I had to do something soon before she hurt another innocent soul.

My body and mind felt completely drained. I went throughout the cabin making sure all the windows and doors were securely locked. I was still a little nervous about my encounter with the disappearing camper. The weather had turned blissfully cold and the only heat was from the fireplace in the living room, so I decided I would sleep there.

THAT NIGHT the dream I had was the most disturbing of all. I stood in the center of what appeared to be a small village from centuries ago. People dressed in long, black robes surrounded me. I wore a similar robe except mine was white. I couldn't make out their faces. What I assumed to be a man with a low, scruffy voice stood next to me and began to speak. It was then I realized I was standing next to a guillotine with my hand on the lever. I tried to remove my hand, but it was impossible. It was as if I had no control over my own body.

He looked directly at me and asked, "Are you prepared to face the consequences for your actions? Answer yes or no." I was confused. I didn't understand what was happening. Before I could say anything he spoke again, "Are you prepared to lose your soul for eternity, so in turn you can take another? Answer yes or no." It was then I realized there was a body laying on the guillotine. I recognized this person; it was my mother. A feeling of utmost pleasure ran through my entire body. I was now in complete control over her life. In an instant my arm began to come down and the lever along with it. It was over. Her lifeless body lay on the guillotine, and blood trickled down her severed neck. Suddenly, I was standing alone. The feeling of pleasure in my body was gone, replaced by complete numbness. I looked down and my robe had turned completely black.

When I first awoke from my dream I couldn't move. I felt like I was paralyzed. As the feeling came back into my body, I experienced an excruciating pain in my chest. What felt like an eternity lasted only a few seconds then it was gone. Never had I experienced anything like that before. I didn't want to know if there was any meaning to this dream. I wanted to forget it. I was sure there must be a reasonable explanation for the pain I had felt. I knew my body was stressed, and I wasn't eating much lately. I convinced myself that the nightmares and the hallucinations I had been having were probably brought on by my own physical neglect.

I decided since I was already awake, I would go for a drive and try to clear my head. When I opened the front door I got a surprise. Everything was covered with a blanket of snow. It must have been snowing for some time because there was already a few inches on the ground. I decided to head into town before it got any worse and stock up on a few things.

I wasn't far from the cabin when I saw someone trudging through the snow just ahead. As I got closer it appeared to be a man waving his arms in the air. I slowed down as I drove up next to him, and then realized it was the camper from the woods. I felt like I should stop and see if he needed help, after all he had come to my rescue. Pulling up beside him, I opened the car door. "Would you like a lift? I'm heading into town," I asked.

"Yes, miss. I most definitely would be grateful," he replied.

Curious as to where his camping buddies were I said, "I see you're alone. Did your hiking friends leave without you?"

Eluding the question as if he didn't hear what I had asked, he said, "You know, sometimes you just have to go it alone. Sometimes that's the only way to face your fears. Being alone sometimes is the only way to see things clearly. Do you know what I mean?"

"I guess that depends on what you're afraid of," I answered, not knowing for sure what he was getting at.

"Have you ever started to make a decision and then at the last second changed your mind, only to see the outcome changed your destiny, and possibly someone else's?"

"I'm not sure what you're getting at. Did something like that happen to you?" I have to admit I was intrigued by his questions.

He began to tell me a story. He said he and some other climbers were scaling a mountain one time, and one of the men climbing close to him ran into some trouble. The man lost his footing and was hanging on for life. He said it just so happened he knew this man. The man had done some very bad things in his past to some people that he knew and cared about, although he had never been able to prove it. As he sat there holding onto him while his body dangled over the cliff, he had thoughts of how easy it would be to just let him fall to his death.

Then a voice inside of him asked if he was prepared to face the consequences of his actions. This conversation was beginning to sound very familiar to me. He made the decision to save him and was thankful that he had. Shortly after that, the man went on to confess his sins and to make things right with the people he had hurt. He said in a strange way, by saving the other man's life, in the process he had saved his own.

The stranger apologized for babbling on and thanked me for the lift to town. As I drove away I couldn't help but think of the similarities between the stranger's life-changing experience and my own disturbing dreams. Still, I would not believe that any of these strange things that were happening to me were anything other than coincidental.

CHAPTER 14

I hadn't seen or spoken to Ella since my father's death. I thought it was time I paid her a visit. As I drove up in front of the house I noticed a strange vehicle parked in the driveway. I made my way up to the door and went inside. It was deathly quiet, but as I started up the stairs I could hear voices coming from my mother's bedroom. At first I thought she was in pain, but soon it was quite clear. The moaning sounds I heard were from pleasure. I pushed the door open to find my father's best friend and my mother in bed together. The same bed my father had died in just a short time ago.

She began yelling and cursing at me to get out. I had never felt such rage and disgust. It didn't take long for her lover to excuse himself, leaving only the two of us. I calmed Ella down by telling her not to be embarrassed. I stressed to her it was my fault.

"Ella, I should have called first. I should have never intruded."

"That's always been your problem. You have no respect for me and you never have," she snapped back.

"You're right," I said. "I've never thought about your feelings like I should have. I know you must be lonely with Father gone."

Nervously pulling her robe around her tightly, she turned away and said, "I was lonely when your father was here. He never really understood me. He always judged me, just like you all did. He wasn't strong enough to reprimand you children, so it was left up to me."

I knew then why she turned away when she spoke. She couldn't look at me and say those lies. She knew I could see right through her. I knew I had to do some talking if I wanted her to believe that I was sympathetic and understanding, so I put on a sincere face and almost choked from what I was about to say.

"Once again, you're right, Ella. Father was weak, and it was wrong for you to have all the responsibility of us children on you. None of us really ever understood you; we just didn't take the time. I would like to take the time now if you will let me. Maybe we could spend some time alone together and get to know one another."

I told her I had been staying at the cabin and while there I found an insurance policy of our father's. I said that I was also quite lonely. I suggested she could drive back with me and take a look at it. I knew she wouldn't pass up the chance if she thought it involved more money. And I was very convincing. I had learned from the best.

I now knew what needed to be done. I wasn't going to let her mock my father's death. She had humiliated, hurt, and deceived everyone I loved. I would now be her judge and jury, and the sentence was death. I couldn't remember the last time I felt joy in my life. I lost everyone I loved. My mother chose every part of my life in one way or another. I couldn't find one good reason for living. I was tired of trying. I felt that with Ella out of the way, maybe things would change. I wouldn't have to worry about her hurting the people I loved anymore. I was prepared to die if I must except it wouldn't be alone.

As I drove through the blinding snow thoughts of my childhood came rushing in. Family outings we had all taken together, except they all missed one thing…the love between a mother and her children. The loneliness and the humiliation my mother had caused our family played like a movie projector in my mind. There was something I had to ask her…something I dearly needed to know. I swallowed down the lump in my throat and pushed the words to the surface. "Ella, did you ever really love Father?"

Rolling her eyes, and with a sarcastic grin she said, "What are you talking about…of course I did."

"Do you feel any guilt for Father's death?"

"Your father was responsible for his own actions…not me," she said sharply while gritting her teeth.

"Were my brothers and I responsible for the abuse and neglect that you put us through?" I asked, choking back the tears.

"You kids owe me your life. If not for me none of you would be what you are today," she said without so much as a blink.

"Ella, what happened to you to make you such a bitter, sadistic human being? Is it impossible for you to own up to the fact that you mentally and physically abused your own children?"

"How can you talk to me this way? I never abused you or your brothers. Your father was the one that was never around. I was the one that had to listen to all of you cry and moan. There was never time for me. I always took care of you spoiled children."

"Don't you understand that's what a mother is supposed to do? She is supposed to take care of her children. When you spoil a child you give them more than what they need. Ella, you never came close to giving us a fourth of what we needed. We would have been better off if you had never been there. But Ella, you are right about one thing…you have made me what I have become: a monster."

I had heard everything I needed to hear. There wasn't anything she could say to justify the things she did. Nothing that bad could have happened to her to cause her to be so evil. That was my opinion. And my opinion was what counted now.

WE NEVER made it to the cabin that night. Ella kept telling me to slow down. The roads had iced over and the snow was blinding. The more she preached the faster I went. Then she said, "Slow down, you're going to kill us."

The last thing I remember saying to her was, "If you believe in God, now would be a good time to start praying." When the car finally stopped rolling there was dead silence.

EPILOGUE

Strangely, I didn't feel any pain. I was sure it was shock. There was blood everywhere, and I couldn't tell how bad I was hurt. Lying in the seat next to me was nothing but a bloody, crumpled-up body. Ella's head slumped forward, almost severed from her neck. In a bizarre twist as I sat there looking at her, I felt pity that she had never taken responsibility for her actions. She always tried to blame someone else. She wanted to ruin my life so badly that in the process she neglected her own.

At that moment, I realized I had done all those things too. I had been manipulative, deceitful, and self-centered pretty much all my life. I never took responsibility. I blamed Ella for all my cruel actions. Deep down in my soul I always knew I had the power to take control of my life but it was easier not to. I had lived my life no better than my mother. Instead I wasted it.

I could have done something different. But I had made my choice. I chose to take a life. And the answer to the question is *no.* I'm not prepared to face the consequences of my actions. Except now I have no choice.

WHEN YOU visit someone's grave you love, they know you're there. Talk to them. Tell them how much you miss them. They used to visit me. They don't come anymore, although much time has passed.

Don't question if evil lives on after death. It does. And the existence of God is very real. I was given many chances in life to do the right thing except I ignored them. We all have angels trying to lead us in the right path, but you have to open your heart and listen.

Some of them will come to you in your dreams and others will appear as strangers. And forgiveness is as important as breathing. In life I experienced these things, but in death I have to learn how important they really are.

Two people died in the crash that day. Confined to darkness for eternity, together we have to relive every moment over and over of the pain and sorrow we caused in life. Only by the grace of God can we break free of our chains and pray he will deliver us from this hell.

Every day starts out the same. The story never changes. But much like my father's precious rose, we are thorns of an innocent soul.

AUTHOR'S NOTE

It's ironic. In life, Ella and Jennifer were each their own worst enemy. But in death they were closely bound together, each wanting redemption. Ella had the assumption that if you had beauty, wealth, and prestige then everything you wanted would come to you. She was abusive to her children; we assume she was responsible for her husband's death. Although it was never quite clear, there was a high probability she was. She lived her life with no regard for human life. Ella never thought that one day she would be the recipient.

Jennifer, taunted and abused by her mother, was filled with rage and thoughts of revenge. She took none of the responsibility for the pain or grief she had caused in her own life. It was easier to blame her mother. She, like her mother, never believed the day of reckoning would come. Jennifer never accepted the belief or faith in God, even when her appointed angels gave her many signs.

So, are we to believe that faith and forgiveness overpower greed and revenge? If not in life, then surely in death.

Movie poster appears courtesy of Zodiac Entertainment
Design © 2013 Zodiac Entertainment

KEY TO HELL

Cassandra closed the door behind her to room 236 and placed the key on the nightstand by the bed. She had frequented this establishment many times over the past few months, reserving a different room each time. However, on this night, key 236 would either unlock the door to madness or free the way to enlightenment. Wasting no time, she reached into her purse, pulled out a mini recorder, and hit the record button.

"I blame no one for what I'm about to do. I have been living under a cloud of darkness for some time now—a life without meaning or purpose. I cannot find the strength to go on any longer."

Hitting the stop button on the recorder, she pushed the playback button and cringed when she heard not her voice, but a beastly growl followed by a disembodied voice.

"Feed that hunger to drive your soul into hell. Unleash your earthly shackles—prepare to walk a carpet of black blood into my kingdom. For here, firelight will brighten your darkness and you shall have a purpose."

Cassandra threw the recorder across the room. The existence of the ghostly evidence lay scattered across the gleaming, wooden floor. Had she been given a foretaste of what her soul would encounter?

Concerned after several days and unanswered calls to room 236, the hotel desk clerk ordered the 'Do Not Disturb' sign be removed.

The desk clerk entered the room with the housemaid following close behind. "Don't tell me it has happened again?"

"What?"

The desk clerk shook his head in disgust. "Looks like another guest skipped out on us early without paying. You think people would have more respect. And why is it that it's always the guests in room 236 that up and disappear—makes no sense!"

ABOUT THE AUTHOR

At an early age, Barbara Watkins experienced what she refers to as supernatural phenomenon. As a teenager, she kept a diary and documented several disturbing nightmares that were later used as inspiration in her writing.

Barbara loves to evoke a false sense of security and expectation in her writing, leading her readers into a world of the unknown. Her articles on various subjects, short stories, and poetry, have appeared in *The Heartland Writers Guild, 2008 New York Skyline Review*, and several online publications.

Her charitable contributions include supporting the Partner in Hope program through the St. Jude Children's Research Hospital.

She resides in Missouri with her husband of thirty-five years, and her faithful, loving Boxweiler, Hooch. She has three children and ten grandchildren.

26914319R00049

Made in the USA
Charleston, SC
24 February 2014